FAIRY TALE BREAKFASTS
A COOKBOOK FOR
YOUNG READERS AND EATERS

Fairy Tales retold by

Jane Yolen

Recipes by

Heidi E.Y. Stemple

Illustrations by

Philippe Béha

alphabet soup™

an imprint of
WINDMILL BOOKS™
New York

For my daughter, for meals cooked, jokes shared, and love always
—JY

For Jen and the thousands of dinners we cooked together, for Nina whose name should be on this book for all the help she gave me, and for all my taste testers especially my daughters—Maddison and Glendon
—HEYS

For my daughters Sara and Fanny
—PB

The recipes in this book are intended to be prepared with an adult's help.

Published in 2010 by Windmill Books, LLC
303 Park Avenue South, Suite # 1280, New York, NY 10010-3657

Adaptations to school & library edition © 2010 Windmill Books
Adapted from *Fairy Tale Feasts: A Literary Cookbook for Young Readers and Eaters.*
Published by arrangement with Crocodile Books, an imprint of Interlink Publishing Group, Inc.

Text copyright © 2006 Jane Yolen and Heidi E. Y. Stemple
Illustrations copyright © 2006 Philippe Béha

Publisher Cataloging Data

Yolen, Jane
      Fairy tale breakfasts : a cookbook for young readers and eaters. – School & library ed. / fairy tales retold by Jane Yolen ; recipes by Heidi E. Y. Stemple ; illustrations by Philippe Béha.
          p. cm. – (Fairy tale cookbooks)
      Contents: The magic pot of porridge–The brewery of eggshells–Diamonds and toads–The runaway pancake.
      Summary: This book includes retellings of four fairy tales paired with breakfast recipes connected to each story.
      ISBN 978-1-60754-573-6 (lib.) – ISBN 978-1-60754-574-3 (pbk.)
ISBN 978-1-60754-575-0 (6-pack)
      1. Cookery–Juvenile literature   2. Breakfasts–Juvenile literature   3. Fairy tales   [1. Cookery   2. Breakfasts
3. Fairy tales]   I. Stemple, Heidi E. Y.   II. Béha, Philippe   III. Title   IV. Series
      641.5/123–dc22

Manufactured in the United States of America.

TABLE OF CONTENTS

STORIES AND STOVETOPS: AN INTRODUCTION

From the earliest days of stories, when hunters came home from the hunt to tell of their exploits around the campfire while gnawing on a leg of beast, to the era of kings in castles listening to the storyteller at the royal dinner feast, to the time of TV dinners when whole families gathered to eat and watch movies together, stories and eating have been close companions.

So it is not unusual that folk stories are often about food: Jack's milk cow traded for beans, Snow White given a poisoned apple, a pancake running away from those who would eat it.

But there is something more—and this is about the powerful ties between stories and recipes. Both are changeable, suiting the need of the maker and the consumer. A storyteller never tells the same story twice, because every audience needs a slightly different story, depending upon the season or the time of day, the restlessness of the youngest listener, or how appropriate a tale is to what has just happened in the storyteller's world. And every cook knows that a recipe changes according to the time of day, the weather, the altitude, the number of grains in the level teaspoonful, the ingredients found (or not found) in the cupboard or refrigerator, the tastes or allergies of the dinner guests, even the cook's own feelings about the look of the batter.

So if you want to tell these stories yourself or make these recipes yourself, be playful. After first making them exactly as they are in this book, you can begin to experiment. Recipes, like stories, are made more beautiful by what *you* add to them. Add, subtract, change, try new ways. We have, and we expect you will, too. In fact, in the recipes, we have already given you some alternatives, like different toppings and other spices.

–Jane Yolen and Heidi E. Y. Stemple

THE MAGIC POT OF PORRIDGE

There was once a poor but good girl named Grete, who lived all alone with her mother by the side of a great forest. Times had been hard and there was nothing left in their cupboards to eat, so Grete decided on her own to go into the forest to look for food.

As she was wandering through the deep woods, she met an old woman who seemed to know exactly what was the matter.

"You are hungry, child?"

Grete curtsied and nodded. "I am hungry, good frau. But not as hungry as my dear mother."

The old fairy—for, of course, she was such—smiled and handed Grete a pot, saying "Take this and instruct it, 'Cook, little pot, cook.' It will give you as much sweet porridge as you and your mother can eat. And when you are full, tell it, 'Stop, little pot, stop.' And it will immediately cease to cook."

Grete took the pot and gazed down into its shiny surface. When she looked up again to thank the old woman, she had vanished.

Now Grete knew better than to shrug off a fairy's blessing, so she took the pot right home to her mother. She set the pot on the

Published by the Brothers Grimm as "Sweet Porridge," this story is part of a whole group of tales known as "magic pot" stories. It is filed in the famous Aarne-Thompson tale type index as type 565. Companion tales to this are the Norwegian "Mill That Grinds Salt at the Bottom of the Sea," and all the Sorcerer's Apprentice stories.

stove and said the magic words and the pot cooked them sweet porridge until they could eat no more.

The next morning Grete went out again into the forest, to try and find the old woman to thank her, leaving the pot at home with her mother.

Now her mother was feeling a bit peckish—which is to say, hunger pangs pecked at her belly again. So she turned to the pot on the stove and said—as her daughter had, "Cook, little pot, cook."

At once the little pot cooked up some wonderful sweet porridge and the mother soon ate her fill. But she hadn't listened carefully to her daughter's instructions on how to stop the pot, and so she cried out, "Enough!"

The pot did not listen, of course, and keep cooking merrily away.

Then the mother began to cry out everything she could think of—"Cease, pot! Enough! Stop cooking! That's plenty! Help!"

But the pot kept cooking more and more porridge.

The porridge filled the pot, rose over the edge, spilled onto the stove, over onto the floor.

"Stop it, pot!" the frantic mother cried. "That's too much! Oh dear, oh dear, oh dear!"

The pot kept cooking.

Porridge filled up the kitchen and then the house, went along the lane to the next house, filled *it* up with porridge and then continued on down the street.

The mother ran out crying for help.

The people in the next house went crying for help.

The people in the village went crying for help.

Finally little Grete came home from the forest and realized what had happened.

"Stop, little pot, stop!" she called.

The pot stopped cooking.

And everyone who wanted to go home had to eat their way back. ★

The grinding mill tale has been found in various tellings from Norway, all the way through Central Europe and down into Greece. It made its way to America, China, and Japan. The famous children's book writer and illustrator Tomie dePaola did his own version, Strega Nona, *which he set in Italy with a magic pasta pot and a silly hero named Big Anthony.*

Perfect Porridge

So good, you'll want more than one bowl. (Makes an individual serving)

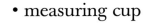

EQUIPMENT:
- measuring cup
- pan
- wooden spoon

INGREDIENTS:
- 1 cup water (230 ml)
- ½ cup oats (40 g)
- dash salt

DIRECTIONS:

1. For each large serving, pour 1 cup of water and a dash of salt into the pan over high heat and bring to a boil.

2. Once water boils, pour in the oats.

3. Turn heat down to medium-high, and stir for 5 minutes, to keep from having lumpy porridge.

4. Serve with salt and milk like the Scots do, or with your favorite toppings (see variations).

NOTE:

For each additional serving, use another cup (230 ml) of water and ½ cup (40 g) of oats.

Facts about porridge:
1. Porridge is another word for oatmeal, which is made of boiled oats. Children throughout Europe, both rich and poor, ate it for breakfast, but rich children had sugar and cream with their porridge. Poor children ate it with skimmed milk (milk with the cream skimmed off the top) and treacle, a kind of molasses.
2. In the old days, porridge was eaten with a wooden spoon, because metal spoons became too hot. The favorite wood for a porridge spoon was birch because it was so easy to keep clean.

VARIATIONS:

Many Americans (and probably Scots, too) like a sweeter porridge.

1. Maple and Brown Sugar: Top with 1 tablespoon maple syrup, 1 tablespoon brown sugar, and a dollop of milk or cream.

2. Butter and Brown Sugar: Top with 1 tablespoon butter and 1 tablespoon brown sugar and a dollop of milk or cream.

3. Bananas and Cream: Mash half a banana with a fork in your bowl. Add 1 tablespoon milk or cream. Add to hot porridge.

4. Apples and Cinnamon: Cut half an apple into small cubes and add to the boiling water with the oats. When cooked, add a tablespoon sugar and ¼ teaspoon cinnamon. Top with a dollop of cream or milk.

5. Raisins and Spice: Add a heaping tablespoon raisins to cooking oats. When cooked, add ¼ teaspoon cinnamon and a dash of ground nutmeg. Top with a dollop of cream or milk.

6. Holiday Porridge: Mix together ¼ cup (60 ml) eggnog with a dash of cinnamon, nutmeg, and cloves. Add to cooked porridge. 🍎

3. Scottish porridge makers use a "spurtle," a little wooden stick, to stir their porridge. They always stir it to the right, not the left, which is considered bad luck.
4. Scottish soldiers often carried little bags of oats with them for a hearty hot meal that could be cooked quickly in boiling water over a campfire.

THE BREWERY OF EGGSHELLS

Once not so long ago, a certain Eileen Murphy gave birth to a baby boy she named Tam. He was a big, healthy, smiling child with bright blue eyes, and a dimple in his chin. At least he was that way on Saturday night when she tucked him into his cradle.

On Sunday morning, before church, he had become a shriveled, squalling, scrawny infant.

"Heavens preserve us!" cried Mrs. Murphy, "the Good Folk have come and exchanged one of theirs for mine, for surely that is a changeling child and not my Tam."

Her friends told her what to do, for it was well known how to treat an imp. "Roast it on a griddle," said one. "Grab its nose with hot iron tongs," said another. "Throw it in the snow," said a third.

But she could not bear to treat the changeling badly. It was a baby, after all, even though it was a devilish child who cried from morning to night and would not be comforted.

So it went for ten days until Mrs. Murphy and her husband were fair exhausted by the babe. And then, as luck would have it—good, bad, and otherwise—Grey Ellen came calling.

Now Grey Ellen was a wise woman of the kind rarely seen today.

She knew all the fairy lore, not just a smattering, and had what is called the "gift." She wandered the countryside, going door to door, helping folk who needed it and even those who did not. Nowadays we would call her a beggar and shoo her away, but then she was fed for a blessing, and given shelter for her wisdom.

"Good day to you, Eileen Murphy," said Grey Ellen.

"Good day it may be," replied Mrs. Murphy, "but for the changeling child who lies in my own Tam's cradle." As she spoke, the changeling set up an awful wail, high as a rabbit's scream.

"Ah," said Grey Ellen, putting a finger aside her nose. "And you cannot bring yourself to roast it or toast it or grab its nose with tongs."

Mrs. Murphy shook her head.

"And this being a summer's day, there's no snow in which to toss it."

Mrs. Murphy nodded her head.

"Then I know just the thing," said Grey Ellen. "Just do as I bid you, and all will be well."

"You will not hurt the poor thing?" asked Mrs. Murphy, her heart full of fear.

Grey Ellen smiled. "I will not, for is it not a child of the Fair Folk? But this is what you must do." And she told her.

Mrs. Murphy gave Grey Ellen a fine tea, with three different kinds of cakes in thanks. Then off went Grey Ellen to help someone else, and into the nursery went Mrs. Murphy.

She brought the child out into the main room of the cottage and laid the baby in a basket by the fire. Then she put a big pot of water on to boil.

The changeling followed her with its big, dark eyes.

Next Mrs. Murphy got out a dozen new-laid eggs, broke them, threw away the insides, and put the shells into the boiling water.

"Yum . . ." she said, "and don't these eggshells smell fine."

Now the baby had been quietly watching everything with great interest for about a quarter of an hour. Suddenly it opened its mouth. But instead of wailing, it said in an old man's voice, "What are you doing, Mommy?"

Mrs. Murphy nearly died of fright that a ten-day-old child should speak, but she answered as Grey Ellen had advised her. "I'm brewing, my son."

"And what are you brewing, Mommy?" asked the child, sitting up in the basket. There was now no question it was a fairy, for surely no ten-day-old baby could do such a thing.

"Eggshells," said Mrs. Murphy. "I'm brewing eggshells."

"Oh!" cried the imp, clapping its tiny hands. "I'm a thousand years in this world and I never saw a brewery of eggshells before!" He leaped up out of the basket, turned around three times on the floor, and disappeared.

A tiny sound came from the basket. Mrs. Murphy ran over to look and there was her little Tam, all sweet-smelling and smiles, bright blue eyes and a dimple in his chin, looking up at her. And never again were the Murphys bothered by the fairies. ⭐

EGGS IN A CRADLE

Because you wouldn't want to eat eggshells for breakfast.

(Makes 3 servings)

EQUIPMENT:
- medium sized cup or glass
- butter knife
- spatula
- griddle (or large skillet)

INGREDIENTS:
- 3 eggs
- 3 pieces of bread
- butter (soft is best)
- salt and pepper
- sliced cheese (optional)

DIRECTIONS

1. Place each piece of bread on a flat surface and put the cup on top of it—upside down. If you cannot see the outside of the bread on all sides, the cup is too big.

2. Gently press the cup down, twisting a bit, to cut out a circle in the middle of each slice of bread. These are your egg cradles. Repeat on each slice of bread. Save the middle rounds for the birds or for eating later.

3. Butter both sides of the cradles. Hint: If your butter is hard from the refrigerator, it will break the bread. Better to melt enough butter in the pan to coat it instead.

4. Warm up the griddle to a medium heat. Place the cradles in it. Drop a small amount of butter into the hole of each (about ¼ tablespoon) unless you have buttered the whole pan.

5. Carefully crack an egg into each cradle.

6. Cook until firm on the cooking side and milky (no longer clear) on the side up.

7. Flip each piece. Hint: make sure to get the spatula under as much of the center egg section as possible or the egg may not hold together.

8. If you want, you may *tuck in* each egg with a slice of cheese.

9. Cook for only a minute or two so as not to overcook the yolk. If you wish to have a solid yolk, pierce it with a fork or the sharp edge of the eggshell as soon as you crack it into the bread in step 5.

10. Serve with salt and pepper.

4. When an egg is laid, it is warm.
5. Albumen is another name for the egg white. It contains 67 percent of the egg's liquid weight and half of its protein.
6. Eggs were not an important part of human diets until Roman times.

DIAMONDS AND TOADS

There was once a widow with two daughters. Now, the oldest daughter was like her mother: ugly and arrogant and mean. The youngest daughter was sweet and kind and lovely. She took after her dear, dead father.

Of course, the widow favored the older daughter, whom she called a gem, and hated the youngest. She gave her the nickname of Slop Girl and made her do all the kitchen work, and all the sweeping and fetching and carrying.

Now one day, in order to punish Slop Girl even more than usual, the widow called her over and said, "Our well is running dry. I want you to go deep into the forest where there is a clear stream and draw our water from that."

Slop Girl nodded.

"And as you will be gone all morning, you can carry a crust of *pain perdu*, day-old bread, with you."

Slop Girl nodded again, took the crust of bread gratefully, and put it in her apron pocket. She walked and walked for several hours before she found the stream. Sitting down on a rock, she

19

began to eat her crust of bread so that she might have energy to draw out the water.

Just then she saw a poor old woman coming along the road, bent over a hawthorn staff.

The old woman sat down next to her and sighed. "I haven't eaten for days," she said.

Slop Girl held out the crust. "It's all I have, but you are welcome to it," she said. "And I will draw some water from the stream so you may drink as well." And she did so with such sweetness that the old woman smiled saying, "Kindness is always rewarded, child. The gift I shall give you is that every word you speak from now on will be accompanied by diamonds and pearls." And she was suddenly gone.

Slop Girl filled the pitcher again and hurried home where her mother scolded her for being late.

"I am so sorry. . ." Slop Girl began, and two diamonds and two pearls suddenly appeared with her words.

Her mother was so stunned by this, she encouraged Slop Girl to tell her the whole story, which was about a hundred and fifty more jewels.

No sooner had she understood the story, then the mother sent for her older daughter, the one upon whom she lavished all her love. She gave her a round of fresh bread and a tiny pitcher and sent her off into the woods, though the girl complained the entire way.

This French folktale is sometimes called "The Fairies" and sometimes called "Slop Girl" after the name of the main character. It is part of a long European tradition of stories in which good and bad sisters are rewarded for the way they act toward little old (disguised) fairies in the woods. There are versions of this story in more than twenty countries.

Of course having toads come out of your mouth every time you say something is disgusting. But diamonds and pearls could make speaking difficult as well. You certainly would want to weigh each thought carefully before saying anything.

But when the old fairy (who else could it be?) came along, bent over a hawthorn stick, the older sister would give her neither a bit of the bread nor a drink from the pitcher. She said instead, "I am not your servant, old lady. So just give me my gift and be gone!"

The fairy nodded and her mouth twisted about. "A gift to suit you indeed," she said. "Every time you speak, your cruel and poisonous words will be accompanied by toads."

The older sister did not believe her until she got home. And then she started to say, "Mama, you would not believe how awful that old lady was. And how smelly!" Fourteen foul toads dropped from her mouth, some as small as pennies and some as big as apples.

Frightened, the widow ran off and her elder daughter after her, crying, "Mama, it's not my fault. . ."–which meant another five toads.

"You are right, my poor pet," cried the mother, "it's Slop Girl's fault." They turned back and beat the poor youngest sister black and blue, until she ran out of the house weeping.

There along the road came a handsome prince who fell in love with Slop Girl before she even spoke a word. And of course he loved her even more after. ⭐

This particular story comes from the Charles Perrault collection of fairy tales, compiled in 1697. Perrault was not writing for children. He was using folktales to talk about the nature of the French court of his day. An earlier version of the story had already appeared in the 1634 Italian collection, Pentamarone. *About that old fairy–sometimes the reward-giver in the story is God accompanied by three angels.*

Very French Toast

A gem of a breakfast. (Makes 3 servings)

EQUIPMENT:
- bowl
- fork
- measuring spoons
- griddle (or large skillet)
- spatula

INGREDIENTS:
- 6 slices of bread
- 4 eggs
- 1 tbsp. cream or milk
- 1 tsp. vanilla
- 1 tbsp. sugar
- ½ tsp. cinnamon
- ¼ tsp. nutmeg
- butter
- syrup (maple, strawberry, blueberry, raspberry—your choice)

DIRECTIONS:

1. Crack the eggs into the bowl. Using the fork, beat the eggs.

2. Add cream and vanilla and beat together.

3. Add the sugar and spices and beat together.

4. Heat the griddle to a medium-high heat and melt approximately 2 tablespoons of butter–enough to coat the entire bottom. Cooking oil can be substituted here (approximately 1 tablespoon).

5. Dip each piece of bread into the egg mixture, coating both sides. You can use your fingers and the fork. Do this quickly so as not to soak in too much mixture, but make sure each piece is thoroughly coated.

6. Place dipped slices on the griddle and cook until golden brown.

7. Flip each piece with the spatula in the order you put them on.

8. When the French toast is golden brown on both sides, remove pieces (two to a plate) and serve with butter and syrup.

4. The British version of French Toast is called "poor knight's pudding" or the "poor knights of Windsor" because it is a cheap meal made by sandwiching jam or syrup between two slices of battered and browned bread. The Germans similarly call the dish arme Ritter, *or poor knights.*
5. The Dutch call this dish wentelteefjes. *The first part is from a word meaning "soaked." Teefje is an old word for a particular shape of pastry—and refers to a female dog.*

THE RUNAWAY PANCAKE

In old Norway there was once a housewife with seven hungry children: Ole, Rolle, Halvor, Mary, Kirsten, Karen, and Little Peter Gynt.

One day, as she was making pancakes for their meal, she used new milk instead of day-old. When she started frying the pancakes, one lay in the pan, beautiful and thick. The children watched her, and her good husband sat by the fire looking on.

"Oh, Mama, I am so hungry," cried Ole. "Give me a bit of the pancake in the pan."

"Ah, please, Mama," said Rolle.

"Please, dear Mama," said Halvor.

"Please dear darling Mama," said Mary.

"Please dear darling kind Mama," said Kirsten.

"Please dear darling kind and generous Mama," said Karen.

"Please dear darling kind and generous and sweet Mama," said Little Peter Gynt.

Mama sighed. "Wait until it turns itself," she said, though she meant to say, *until I have turned it.* But she was tired and frazzled and not speaking plain.

The pancake heard this, was frightened and excited at once, and tried to climb out of the pan. However, it only turned itself on the other side, where it fried a bit more.

"Halloo," cried Ole, Rolle, Halvor, Mary, Kirsten, Karen, and Little Peter Gynt, "see what the pancake has done."

Mama came over to see, and at that, the pancake, feeling stronger than before, jumped out of the pan and onto the floor, rolling away just like a cart wheel, right through the open door and down the road.

Well, Mama ran after it, frying pan in one hand, ladle in the other. After her went Ole, Rolle, Halvor, Mary, Kirsten, Karen, and Little Peter Gynt, waving their napkins. And the good husband came running last of all, his cane in his hand. All of them shouted for the pancake to stop, which only seemed to make it go faster. Soon it was so far ahead they could no longer see it, and they were so tired, they stopped, turned around, and went home.

But the pancake rolled on and on until it met a bearded man.

"Halloo, pancake," said the man, who was hungry.

"Halloo, Manny Panny," said the pancake.

"Wait a bit, pancake and I will eat you," said the hungry man.

"I have run way from Goody Poody and her old husband and her seven squalling children: Ole, Rolle, Halvor, Mary, Kirsten, Karen, and Little Peter Gynt and I shall run away from you, too."

Off rolled the pancake over the hill and out of sight.

The pancake rolled and rolled until it met a peckish hen.

"Halloo, pancake," said the hen.

"Halloo, Henny Penny," said the pancake.

"Don't roll so fast," said the peckish hen, "for I would love to peck you."

"I have run away from the hungry man, from Goody Poody and her old husband and her seven squalling children: Ole, Rolle, Halvor, Mary, Kirsten, Karen, and Little Peter Gynt. And I shall run away from you, too." Off rolled the pancake over the hill and out of sight.

The pancake rolled and rolled until it met a plucky duck.

In the Scottish version the main character is a bannock, *an oatmeal cake. In Russia, he is a talking bun. There are tales in Germany, Slovenia, and over thirty Irish versions. "The Gingerbread Man", an ever-popular American version of the story, was first published in St. Nicholas Magazine in May 1875. The refrain from the American version is still popular:*

Run, run
as fast as you can,
You can't catch me,
I'm the
Gingerbread Man.

"Halloo, pancake," said the duck.

"Halloo, Ducky Lucky," said the pancake.

"Don't roll so fast," said the plucky duck, "for I would love to pluck you."

"I have run away from the peckish hen, from a hungry man, from Goody Poody and her old husband and her seven squalling children: Ole, Rolle, Halvor, Mary, Kirsten, Karen, and Little Peter Gynt. And I shall run away from you, too." Off rolled the pancake over the hill and out of sight.

The pancake rolled and rolled until it met a portly pig standing near a dark and tangled wood.

"Halloo pancake," said the pig.

"Halloo Piggy Wiggy," said the pancake.

"Don't roll so fast," said the portly pig, "for I am a slow-goer. Let's walk a bit and talk a bit. You look like someone who has seen a lot of the world. If we keep company, we can keep one another safe."

Now the pancake was not, in fact, someone who had seen much of the world. And the woods did, indeed, look dark and dangerous. So he decided to travel with the portly pig until they came to a little river.

"I can swim over," said the pig, "and carry you on my back. Otherwise you will get all wet and fall to pieces."

So the pancake climbed upon the pig's back. But when they were in the middle of the water, the pig looked over his shoulder and *Snip-Snap!* He ate up the pancake in one easy bite. Which is the end of the story. And the end of the pancake as well! ⭐

Runaway Pancakes

Eat them quick before they get away. (Makes 2–4 servings)

EQUIPMENT:

- measuring spoons

- large measuring cup (or medium-sized bowl)

- large spoon or whisk

- large mixing bowl

- large skillet or electric skillet with a top

- spatula

INGREDIENTS:

- 1 cup flour (115 g)

- 1 tbsp. sugar

- 1 tbsp. baking powder

- ¼ tsp. salt

- 1 egg

- 1 cup milk (230 ml)

- 2 tbsp. cooking oil

- extra cooking oil

- butter and syrup

Facts about pancakes:
1. Pancakes probably came originally from China and Nepal. They came to Europe in the twelfth century with Crusaders, who were returning from the Middle East.
2. Many cultures around the world make some type of pancake. The Russian pancake is the blini, made with yeast and spread with sour cream or caviar.
3. The Chinese make scallion pancakes with rolled dough shaped like a snail.

DIRECTIONS:

1. Measure the dry ingredients (flour, sugar, baking soda, and salt) and mix together in the large measuring cup (or bowl). Set aside.

2. Crack the egg into the large mixing bowl and beat. Add milk and oil and mix together.

3. Add the dry ingredients and stir well or whisk until batter is lump-free—not too long. If the batter is too thick or thin, add more milk or flour. The thickness of the batter is up to you: thicker means fluffier pancakes, thinner means crisper pancakes.

4. Heat the griddle or skillet to medium-high heat and pour a small amount of oil (start with the size of the bottom of a coffee mug and add more if needed) and spread it over the entire cooking surface with the spatula.

5. Test the heat by getting a drop of water on your fingers and flicking it onto the cook surface. When the water *dances*, it is ready to cook. If it just sits there, continue heating. But, use only a drop or two so you don't get splashed and burned.

6. Pour or scoop the batter onto the heated cook surface. The amount you use dictates your pancake size.

7. Flip each pancake when the bubbles that come to the uncooked surface pop and remain open.

8. Cook second side until golden.

9. Serve with butter and syrup.

4. In India thin pancakes called chapattis *are cooked on a griddle and used to scoop up curries.*
5. In Britain, on Shrove Tuesday—the end of Lent—people eat pancakes made with sugar and lemon juice.
6. At Chanukah, many Jewish people make potato pancakes called latkes, *which are fried in oil and covered with sour cream or applesauce.*

For more great fiction and nonfiction, go to windmillbooks.com.